The Sweetest Friends

By Amy Acklesberg

SCHOLASTIC INC.

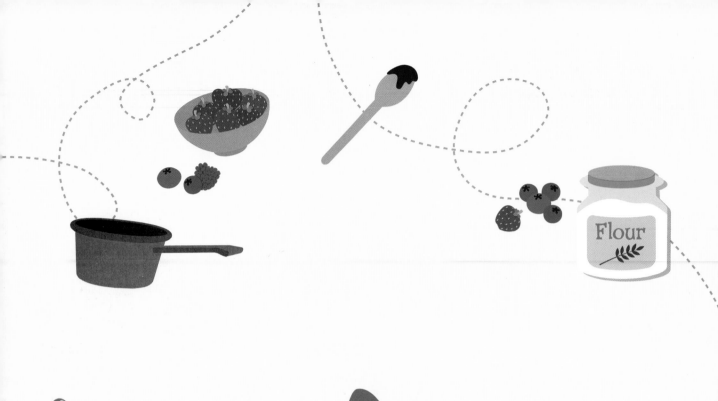

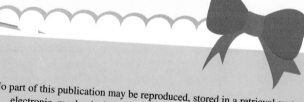

ISBN 978-0-545-53366-9

© 2013 MGA Entertainment, Inc. LALALOOPSY™ is a trademark of MGA in the U.S. and other countries. All logos, names, characters, likenesses, images, slogans, and packaging appearance are the property of MGA.

Used under license by Scholastic Inc. All Rights Reserved.

SCHOLASTIC and associated logos are trademarks and/or registered trademarks of Scholastic Inc.

12 11 10 9 8 7 6 5 4 3 2 1

13 14 15 16 17/0

Cover designed by Angela Jun and Carla Alpert
Interior designed by Angela Jun and Two Red Shoes Design
Printed in the U.S.A.

First printing, November 2013

40

Crumbs Sugar Cookie was baking chocolate banana muffins with her friends Pickles B.L.T. and Toffee Cocoa Cuddles.

"This is so much fun," said Pickles. "We should invite more friends to join us!"

"I know!" said Crumbs. "Let's have a baking contest. Our friends can make yummy treats, and we can be the judges!"

"**W**hat a delicious idea," said Toffee.
"The winner will be the best baker in all of Lalaloopsy Land!" exclaimed Pickles.

Crumbs, Pickles, and Toffee spread the word about the bake-off. Everyone in Lalaloopsy Land was very excited.

Bun Bun Sticky Icing and Twist E. Twirls signed up to bake. So did Cherry Crisp Crust and Toasty Sweet Fluff.

Baking Contest

Rules:
Partner up!

Sign up here!

"I want to be in the contest, too," said Bubble Smack 'N' Pop, "but I've never baked anything before."

"I can help you," said her friend Sugar Fruit Drops. "It'll be fun to work together!"

Bubble and Sugar started to get ready for the contest. They decided to make fruit bars.

"First, you gather the ingredients," Sugar explained. "Then you follow the recipe step-by-step."

"This is so exciting!" exclaimed Bubble as she and Sugar carefully measured and mixed the ingredients.

Together, Bubble and Sugar shaped the dough, cooked the fruit filling, and put the bars into the oven.

"Remember, the oven is hot," said Sugar, putting on her oven mitts. "You need to be very careful when you bake!"

Soon it was time to take the treats out of the oven. "These are delicious!" exclaimed Bubble. "Thanks for teaching me how to make them."

"You're welcome," said Sugar. "I had a great time baking with you!"

Meanwhile, Cherry Crisp Crust and Toasty Sweet Fluff couldn't agree on what to make for the contest.

"I think we should bake a cherry pie," said Cherry. "It's my specialty."

"I don't know," said Toasty. "I was hoping to make my special marshmallow treats."

"*Hmm,*" said Cherry. "What can we bake that would make us both happy?"

"Let's see what ingredients we have," said Toasty. "We have butter, sugar, and cherries."

"Plus flour, marshmallows, and chocolate," said Cherry. "If we combine them, we can make . . ."

"**A** cherry chocolate marshmallow pie!" exclaimed Toasty. "That sounds very tasty!" Cherry said.

"I knew we could think of something great if we worked together," said Toasty.

Bun Bun Sticky Icing and Twist E. Twirls were working hard to make the perfect cinnamon-twist sugar cookies.

The two friends mixed the dough and twirled it into fun shapes.

"Now it's time to bake our creations!" said Twist E. as she popped them into the oven.

But when she took them out . . . the cookies were burned! "Oh, no!" cried Twist E. "This is all my fault!"

"It was an accident," said Bun Bun.

"But we don't have enough flour to make more," said Twist E. "Now we can't enter the contest!"

uddenly, there was a knock at the door. It was Bubble and Sugar. "We smelled something burning," said Bubble. "Is everything okay?" "Our cookies are ruined," said Twist E. sadly. "And we're out of flour."

18

"We can give you some flour," said Sugar.

"But, Sugar, it's supposed to be a contest!" exclaimed Bubble.

"Helping our friends is more important," said Sugar. "We can't let you miss out on the fun!"

"Thank you!" said Bun Bun.

When it was time for the contest, everyone presented their goodies to the judges. Crumbs, Pickles, and Toffee took turns trying the treats.

"We have the results!" said Toffee. "The winner is . . ."

"All of you!" cried Pickles.

"These desserts are so delicious," said Crumbs. "We think each is special in its own way!"

"Hooray!" their friends exclaimed.

Most Creative

"What tasty cookies!" Bubble and Sugar told Bun Bun and Twist E. as they collected their awards.

Bun Bun smiled. "We couldn't have made them without you!"

"Yes," agreed Twist E. "The real winner today is teamwork!"

Crunchiest

Sweetest

The winner is Everybody!

"And now for the best part," said Pickles. "Let's eat!"